THIS CANDLEWICK BOOK BELONGS TO:

_____

_____

_____

_____

For Josie and Oliver

Copyright © 1995 by Lucy Cousins

First U.S. paperback edition 1997

The Library of Congress has cataloged the hardcover edition as follows:

Cousins, Lucy.
Za-Za's baby brother / Lucy Cousins.
Summary: Za-Za the zebra must adjust to the arrival
of a baby brother.
ISBN 1-56402-582-9 (hardcover)
[1. Zebra—Fiction. 2. Babies—Fiction.] I. Title
PZ7.C83175Zaj   1995
[E]—dc20   94-47190

ISBN 0-7636-0337-6 (paperback)

2 4 6 8 10 9 7 5 3 1

Printed in Hong Kong

This book was typeset in Lucy Cousins.
The pictures were done in gouache.

Candlewick Press
2067 Massachusetts Avenue
Cambridge, Massachusetts 02140

Za-Za's
Baby Brother

Lucy Cousins

CANDLEWICK PRESS
CAMBRIDGE, MASSACHUSETTS

My mom is going to have a baby.

She has a big fat tummy. There's not much room for a hug.

Granny came to
take care of me.

Dad took Mom to the hospital.

When the baby was born
we went to see Mom.

When Mom came home
she was very tired.
I had to be very quiet
and help Dad
take care
of her.

All my uncles and aunts came to see the baby.

What a good boy.

Ooh, he's gorgeous.

I played by myself.

Dad was always busy.

Mom was always busy.

"Dad, will you read me a story?"
"Not now, Za-Za. We're going shopping soon."

"Mom, can we go to the toy store?"

"Sorry, Za-Za, the baby's hungry and we have to go home."

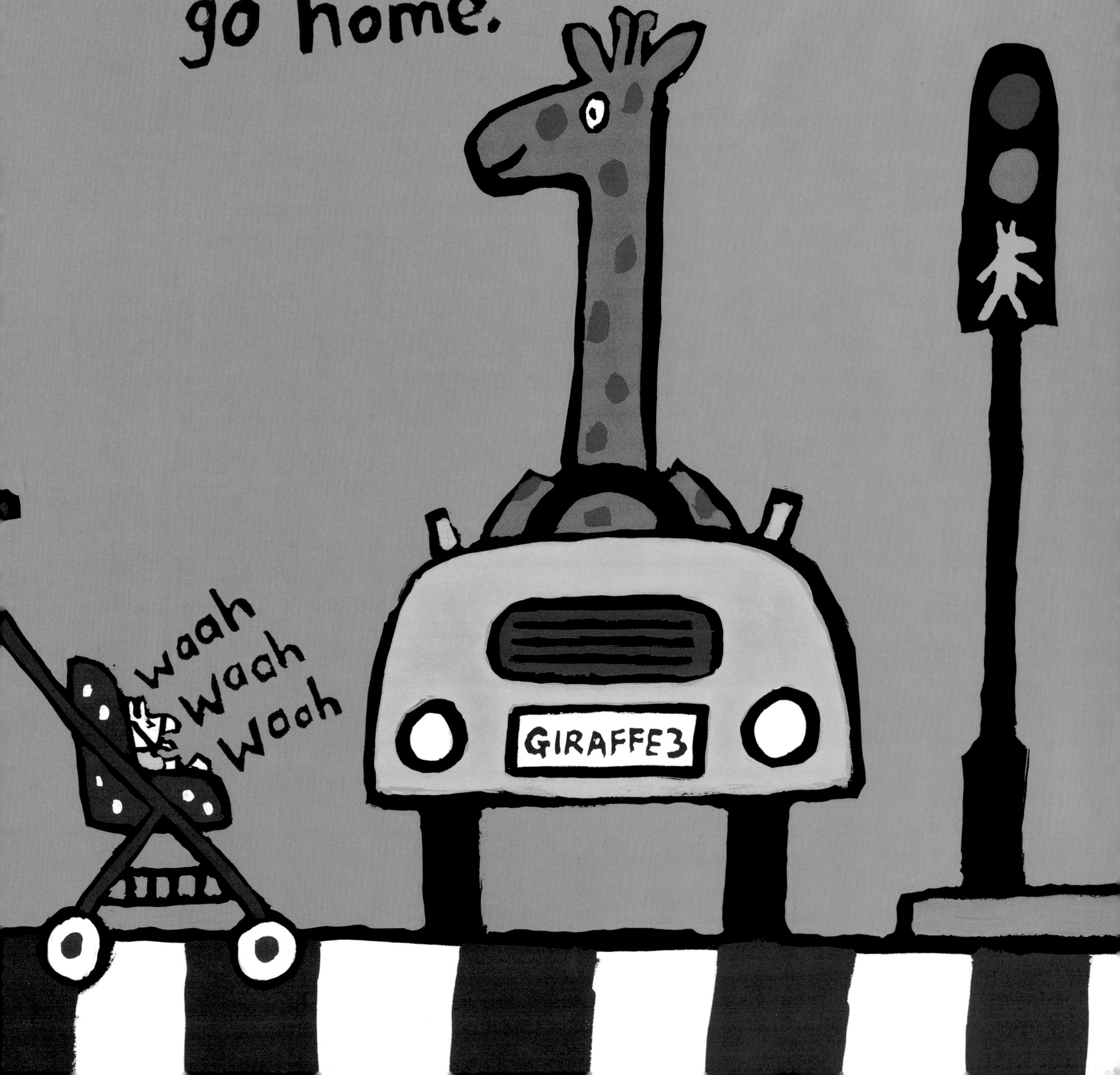

So I hugged the baby...

and I pushed him...

and I built him a tower.

He was nice.
It was fun.

When the baby got tired Mom put him to bed.

Then I got my hug...

and a bedtime story.

Lucy Cousins has been widely acclaimed as one of the most exciting illustrators for children working today. She created *Za-Za's Baby Brother* after her second child was born. "I was really concerned about my older child's feelings since she had been the one and only for three years. I wanted to show the difficulties as well as the fun of having a new baby in the house." Lucy Cousins is now the mother of four children, including, most recently, twins!